T0130133

YOU DESERVE
the Good Things
in Life

Power of Natural Intelligence
and Conscious Energy Flow

JOSEPH & JENNIFER GAMBOA

BALBOA
PRESS
A DIVISION OF HAY HOUSE

Balboa Press books may be ordered through booksellers or by contacting:

Balboa Press
A Division of Hay House
1663 Liberty Drive
Bloomington, IN 47403
www.balboapress.com
1 (877) 407-4847

Because of the dynamic nature of the Internet, any web addresses or links contained in this book may have changed since publication and may no longer be valid. The views expressed in this work are solely those of the author and do not necessarily reflect the views of the publisher, and the publisher hereby disclaims any responsibility for them.

The author of this book does not dispense medical advice or prescribe the use of any technique as a form of treatment for physical, emotional, or medical problems without the advice of a physician, either directly or indirectly. The intent of the author is only to offer information of a general nature to help you in your quest for emotional and spiritual well-being. In the event you use any of the information in this book for yourself, which is your constitutional right, the author and the publisher assume no responsibility for your actions.

(The Message)
-"Scripture taken from The Message. Copyright © 1993, 1994, 1995, 1996, 2000, 2001, 2002. Used by permission of NavPress Publishing Group."

Scripture taken from the King James Version of the Bible.

(NIV)
-THE HOLY BIBLE, NEW INTERNATIONAL VERSION®, NIV® Copyright © 1973, 1978, 1984, 2011 by Biblica, Inc.® Used by permission. All rights reserved worldwide.

(TLB)
-The Living Bible copyright © 1971 by Tyndale House Foundation. Used by permission of Tyndale House Publishers Inc., Carol Stream, Illinois 60188. All rights reserved. The Living Bible, TLB, and the The Living Bible logo are registered trademarks of Tyndale House Publishers.

Any people depicted in stock imagery provided by Thinkstock are models, and such images are being used for illustrative purposes only. Certain stock imagery © Thinkstock.

Print information available on the last page.

ISBN: 978-1-5043-8684-5 (sc)
ISBN: 978-1-5043-8686-9 (hc)
ISBN: 978-1-5043-8685-2 (e)

Library of Congress Control Number: 2017913344

Balboa Press rev. date: 12/20/2017

"No problem can be solved from the level of consciousness that created it."

-Albert Einstein

DEDICATION

I dedicate this book to the inspiration behind my inspirations, my father. He made everything possible for me to share and deliver these thoughts and observations. He is a man filled with the highest intelligence – *"compassion"*. "If you shot him and he survived, he would give the bullets back to you."

I also dedicate this book to you. The simple fact that your hands are embracing it; contributes to the conscious energy freely flowing around us to cancel out and overpower negative thought frequencies in your immediate atmosphere.

Some say that, "the sins of parents follow their children," or that, "when I met the parents, I forgave the children." I believe that the blessings of parents also follow their children. Therefore, we should embrace and receive the blessings of their sacrifices, for most of them, we may never know. There is an ancient Chinese proverb that states, "If you carried your parents on your back for a thousand years in the sand, you could never repay them."

Try to use your energy to be thankful for what you have instead of using this energy for what you desire. This shift in thinking will deliver to your feet more things to be thankful for. Even UPS does not deliver to your feet. This is a privilege reserved for Kings and Queens. We are all in this together on this dirt rock; whether we like it or not. We might as well enjoy the dance while the music is playing. Joseph…

TABLE OF CONTENTS

PREFACE

The motivation of this volume is to share and express ancient and modern unconventional observations of energy and intelligence; infinite sources that surround us in our Natural World, that with the right understanding and proper application will harmoniously serve others and ourselves as we occupy our environment.

It is a collective of sciences and thoughts gathered to teach and inspire a higher level of awareness and consciousness. To ignite the Divine impulse that dwells deep within all of us for a specific and significant purpose so that we may evolve on a physical, mental, and spiritual plain.

This is the *Pocket Power Book* version and has been formatted to be utilized as a tool. The preselected images contained in it correspond to the following chapter. Once you can relate and interpret the image with the principle, then you are ready to move on to the next chapter.

INTRODUCTION

It was when I was in the first grade, sitting on an old wooden classroom floor, in an old brick building, located on an old street, in an old neighborhood, in an old city, peering into an old book, with a new idea.

"Chug, chug, chug. Puff, puff, puff. Ding-dong, ding-dong. The little train rumbled over the track. She was a happy little train." She was called 'The Pony Engine' in the book "*The Little Engine That Could*" by Watty Piper.

"That's correct, you can do it," said Mrs. Gotlieb, as I attempted to read my first book from cover to cover. "I think I can, I think I can. Chug, chug, chug, puff, puff, puff. I think I can, I think I can." By the time, I reached the end of the book, the *new* words, "*I think I can, I think I can,*" were repeatedly playing in my head like an old, scratched 'Monkeys' album.

Later on, that evening as we sat at the dinner table, my father gave the usual command, "pass the salad." I looked at him with a silly grin and responded, "I think I can, I think I can."

Like a steady droplet of water on a stone, back up your intended thought, with the same thought, repeatedly. Just as the words in the classic book stated, "*I think I can, I think I can.*" As the water droplet will eventually penetrate through the stone, your intended thought will break through the lower thought to reach the higher desired frequency.

We have access to frequencies that transmit our intentions on various waves. It is like turning a dial on a radio, one station at a time until you reach a clear reception. You know the one; when all the green bars jump to the top. But you normally don't just settle for the first clear station that you pick up. You keep going, and going, until finally you reach the *intended* and *desired* music. Now what do you do? You PUMP up the volume!

There are more people on the Earth on the negative plain of thought than on the positive plain, and consequently there are more negative thought vibrations in effect in our atmosphere. But, happily for us we can counterbalance this by the fact that a positive thought is infinitely more powerful than a negative one, and by a strong determined force of will, if we raise ourselves to a higher mental state we can shut down the depressing thoughts and engage in the charged vibrations with our changed mental attitude. We may also get the positive thought-waves of others on the same plain of thought.

Do not allow yourself to be affected by the negative thoughts of those around you. Rise to the upper chambers of your mental dwelling, and amp yourself up to a strong vibration, way above the vibrations on the lower plains of thought and you will be surprised at what you discover. Then you will not only be immune to their negative vibrations but will be in touch with the great body of strong thoughts coming from those of your plain of development.

This book was developed from years of research on a collective of thoughts, and I will attempt to give you the working principles, expressions of wisdom, and exercises, leaving it up to you to apply them for yourself, rather than attempting to teach it in detail. If you follow them and pay attention, you will be able to work out and apply these principles. If you do not you must develop yourself any way that you can; otherwise it will just be words. That is all, just words. Let us explore the mastery of your mind, the transformation of one kind of mental vibration into other mental vibrations.

As well-advanced mind transformers have the ability to obtain the degree of power necessary to even control physical conditions that control the elements of nature; the sensation of earthquakes or the senses and other physical phenomenon. These mind masters they do not make public expositions of their powers. They stay away from crowds of men to better work their way along the path of attainment.

This is only mentioned to you for you to recognize that the power is entirely in your mind and operates along the lines of a higher mind transformation.

"Let us learn and practice what we instinctively know to be a fact; namely that the present-day generation and misery of the human race cannot be alleviated by laws and regulations, by loans and covenants, but improvement must come from within ourselves; it must come through a complete rebirth; through different mental attitude, different conception and conduct of life; through return of naturalness, true religion, simplicity, frugality, economy and joyous renunciation; through up building and uplifting; through honesty and tolerance; through purposeful strengthening of body, mind and soul, so that we will again feel throbbing life within us, strong and powerful, enabling us to again enjoy life, nature, family life, art, books, pictures and songs, and to bear bravely whatever pains and vicissitudes life holds in store for us."

CHAPTER 1

The Nature of the Force

J UST AS YOU can change water to ice and ice back to water, so you can do the same with your mind. Before any of your muscles can respond, a mental activity must take place. It all starts in the mind. Before the creation of the Universe, it must have been a thought in the mind of the Creator. Therefore, we must be able to create our world, or our universe with a thought in our mind.

"Transmute" means "to change from one nature, form or substance, into a higher form; to transform" (Webster). The mind, as well as, any other form of matter may be transformed from one degree to another degree, from one end of the spectrum to the other end of the spectrum, from vibration to vibration to vibration. With today's available technology we can now create and manufacture diamonds from human hair in an office building. They are virtually real GIA certifiable diamonds. This is done by extracting the carbon from human remains and subjecting them to the same conditions, temperatures and pressures in which coal is transformed into diamonds in the natural world. If we can transform the world's hardest material, then we possess the ability to transform our minds under any condition.

This principle suggests that the underlying reality of the Universe is thought. If it is mental in nature, then mind transformation must be the ability to change the conditions in our lives, in our environment and in our world. I often recommend that if you want to lose weight, altering your diet is not always the most effective method. We tend to put the weight back on; however, if you purify and change your mind, you no longer desire impure things. Ultimately, this cleanses the body of toxins, unhealthy desires and habits. Then the body will naturally restore itself to its optimal state.

"Where the mind goes, the body soon follows."

It is also possible to unconsciously transform the mental states of others. Remember the scene in *Star Wars,* when the young Obi-Wan

Kenobi while looking for an assassin, took a seat in a bar next to an alien patron?

> The Patron asked Obi-Wan, "Do you want to buy some death sticks?"
> Obi-Wan waved his hand and replied, "You do not want to sell me death sticks."
> Patron replied "I do not want to sell you death sticks."
> Obi-Wan continued "You want to go home and re-think your life."
> Patron responds with "I want to go home and re-think my life." Confused, the yielded Patron turns and walks away.

Like a stone thrown into the water, thoughts produce ripples and waves which spread out over the great ocean of thought. There is a difference, however; the waves on the water move only on a level plain in all directions, whereas thought-waves move in all directions from a common center, just as the rays from the sun.

On Earth, we are surrounded by a great sea of Minds. Our thought-waves extend through this vast sea in all directions. They resemble sound waves and have the property of reproducing themselves. Just as a note of the violin will cause the thin glass to vibrate and "sing," so will a strong thought tend to awaken similar vibrations and minds attuned to receive it. Many of the stray thoughts that come to us are but reflections or answering vibrations to some strong thought sent by another. But unless our minds are attuned to receive it, the thought will not likely affect us. If we are thinking high and great thoughts, our minds acquire a certain keynote similar to the character of the thoughts we are thinking. And, this keynote once established, we will be able to catch the vibrations of other minds keyed to that same thought. If we get into the habit of thinking negative thoughts, we will soon be reflecting the low frequencies from the minds of the thousands thinking along the same lines.

We have heard this many times before that we are largely what we have thought ourselves into being, the balance being represented by the character of the suggestions and thoughts of others, which have reached us by verbal suggestions, or mentally by means of such thought waves. Our *Attitude* determines the character of the thought-waves received from others, as well as, the thoughts coming from our own minds. We receive only such thoughts that are in harmony with our mental attitude; the thoughts out of harmony with our thoughts will have little effect and they will not influence a response in us.

That which we call personal magnetism, is the subtle current of thought waves projected from the human mind. Every thought created by our minds is a force of greater or lesser intensity, varying in strength according to the person imparted to it at the time of its creation. When we think, we send from us subtle currents which travels along like a ray of light and has its influence on the minds of others who are often far removed from us by space, a forceful thought will go on its errand charged with a mighty power, and will often beat down the instinctive resistance of the minds of others. Whereas a weak thought will be able to obtain an entrance to the mental castle of another, unless the castle is heavily guarded. Repeated thoughts along the same lines, sent often after the other will often affect an entrance where a single thought wave although much stronger will be repulsed.

A steady drip of water will wear down a stone far greater than one giant splash. We are all influenced much more than we are aware of by the thoughts of others. I do not mean their opinions, but their thoughts. A great writer once said, "Thoughts are things." They are things, and most important, powerful things at that. Unless we understand this, we are at the mercy of a mighty force, of whose nature we know nothing, and whose very existence many of us deny. On the other hand, when we understand the laws governing this wonderful force, we gain the ability to yield it and master it, and render it as our instrument and assistant.

We think ourselves into being. The Bible states that, "For as he thinketh in his heart, so is he" is literally correct. (Proverbs 23:7) We are creatures of our own mental creating. You know how easy it is to think yourself into a depressed state of mind; or vice versa. That repeated thought upon a certain line will repeat itself not only in your character, but also in your physical appearance of the thinker as well. Have you ever noticed how a man's occupation shows itself in his appearance and general character? What do you think causes this? Nothing more or less than that thought. If you ever changed your occupation, your general character and appearance kept pace with your changed habits and thoughts. Your new occupation brought a new change of thought, and thought takes form in action.

A man who thinks Energy, manifests Energy. The man, who thinks Courage, manifests Courage. Now, what causes the difference? Just plain everyday thinking is the difference. Thought, that is all. Of course, the action follows the thought. But why? Because it cannot help itself.

Action follows as the natural result of vigorous thinking. Your thought attracts to it the corresponding thoughts of others and increases your **"Stock"** of that particular kind of thought. Do you see the point? Think fearful thoughts and you draw yourself to fear. You draw yourself to yourself all the fear thought in that neighborhood. The harder you think of it, the greater supply of thought flocks to you.

"Illusions"

In the early nineteenth century, for example, a message could travel only as fast as a human being, which on a horse was thirty-five miles per hour.

Our technological ingenuity transformed information into a form of garbage, and ourselves into garbage collectors.

The tie between information and human purpose has been severed. Information is now a commodity that is bought and sold; it comes indiscriminately, whether asked for or not, directed at no one in particular, in enormous volumes, at high speeds, disconnected from meaning and significance. There is an illusion that "we think that we are thinking."

CHAPTER 2

Activating Force

S UCCESS IN LIFE depends very materially upon the possession of attracting and influencing our fellow men or women. Never take "No" for an answer. Pursue the same plan in business that you would if you were chasing after the girl of your dreams. Pursue the same tactics in your business and you will win the day. Suggestions gain force by repetition, just as the continuous water droplets drip to penetrate the old stone. To influence a man with whom you come in personal contact, you will not have to depend entirely upon the power of suggestion to overcome his watchfulness of his mind. You will be aided by two powerful allies, direct waves consciously projected by your mind, and by the involuntary qualities of thought. These powers can be highly developed by continued exercise of these principles.

After my trials and tribulations, the thought was brought to my attention that success in life could be obtained by developing strength of character and controlling my mental forces. Wisdom without Force is of small value. Force without Wisdom, while expanding itself largely is useless and ill directed efforts accomplishes little or nothing. As wisdom increases, the mental forces are conserved and are not driven to excess. They are exercised but not exhausted, which increases the limit of Force. One possessing Wisdom and a small degree of Force, by properly directing that Force, accomplishes more than when he/she has more Force and a lesser degree of Wisdom. Seek Wisdom.

Well laid plans and determined efforts, often bring small returns, while great success is the outgrowth of small beginnings. When Sam Walton, the father and founder of Wal-Mart, opened his first retail store in a small town in Arkansas, he had an ingenious method to get customers to enter his store over the larger competition; popcorn. Yes, popcorn. He would roll his sleeves up and make popcorn all day outside at the front entrance of his store. The fresh buttery smell would lure customers until they were standing around the corner waiting in line. They could not help but to see the low-priced advertisements while waiting for their serving of popcorn.

Considering this, it is easy to determine that physical stature does not have to be the case since some of the world's greatest leaders have been smaller than average men. If you investigate the educational line, few were college bred and some were illiterate. It is evident that the secret lay not in education. Also, some people have the ability to absorb knowledge as easily as a sponge absorbs water, but they are unable to derive any benefit from their learning, while their classmates who are unable to learn often startle the world by some great achievement.

Negative natures make the best students but positive natures produce the most action. Often the most obedient boy or girl in school became a clerk for the worst "rascals." The *educated, independent thinker* was the best of all. The man who was the most anxious to obtain money had the least; his sole ambition was to own a cottage, and he had nothing more. The man who hated the most was loved the least. The man who tried to frighten others, was afraid. If you observe haters their bodies are always tensely drawn, the muscles incapable of relaxing, their minds and bodies are shriveled, functions impaired, and the body full of aches and pains. This explanation is not just for hatred, but jealousy and dependency had an attraction for a mind out of harmony and produced a corresponding effect in the body.

The one who could swear the loudest curse was the one who could run the quickest. That man would become a victim to circumstances, while his brother laughed at the other man's negative surroundings and negative suggestions and "sailed on." Some men talk of doing great things, while others just do them and say nothing. Talkative people could not stop their chatter even if they desired; "The more talk, the less truth; the wise measure their words. Proverbs 10:19 (The Message Bible)." Silent men talk more interestingly than the talkers. Any line of business is a medium for an accumulation of wealth for the right-thinking man.

Considering all these things, it leads us to believe, neither the size of the man nor the learning he possess has anything to do with the accomplishment of his objective, but instead, the condition of his mind together with the desire and expectation of success, seem to attract everything to him. The study of Mind Transformation and the Power of Suggestion shows clearly that confidence concerning one's ability to do something could be developed, and that the belief made the doing possible.

"Know oneself," is the deepest and best advice ever given to mankind. It embraces the knowledge that character of self can be strengthened and distinguished. That force can be added to one; that the mind attracts success in all things as it is freed from fear, jealousy, ill-will, envy, distrust, anger, and haste.

The power and value of the imagination that one grows becomes whatever he/her thinks of himself/herself as being, and is literally what he/she thinks himself/herself into being. A child raised in poverty is always in contact with poor people and sees in their homes, as well as, in his/her own neighborhoods only the bare necessities of life. The child hears how hard it is to get money, knows his father works hard for little wages, wears poor clothing and conforms to all the life of the poor until it becomes a part of him. The evidence he hears of wealth is not real for him. He feels it is not for him. The things he has seen all of his life, the circumstances with which he has been surrounded, have created that frame of mind.

"Embezzlers"

What are some of these embezzlers - those things that drain away our time and resources?

<u>Texting & Twittering</u> - *You just can't seem to let a text message or tweet go unanswered.*

<u>Email Spam</u> - *All those cute stories and poems are entertaining, but who has the time?*

<u>Email Messages</u> - *Wish I had time to do justice to all of them, but …*

<u>Cell phones</u> - *Isn't there any place where it is okay to be out of touch anymore?*

<u>Video games</u> - *I only intended to play for an hour. Where did the evening go?*

<u>Internet</u> – With all its eye-catching images and articles.

<u>Television</u> - *We all say there isn't anything to watch, but we watch it anyway.*

<u>Spectator sports</u> - *When does one more game get to be too much?*

Many of the demands on our time cannot be avoided, but what do we do with the rest of the time? What do we get accomplished in our 24 hours?

Thoughts:_____

_____
_____
_____
_____
_____
_____
_____
_____
_____
_____
_____
_____
_____
_____
_____
_____
_____
_____
_____
_____
_____
_____
_____
_____
_____
_____
_____
_____
_____
_____
_____
_____
_____
_____

Now let them make mental images of themselves occupying a better position in life, having money and friends in everything they desire. In time that becomes the reality, while the old life is the unreal. By changing the mind; it changes the circumstances. They have risen above circumstances and have controlled them.

The study of Nature in all her forms, the effects of desire in animals and humans, prove the existence of the law of vibration, and if the law was invoked vigorously to supply the deficient quality in each mentality their inflow followed. But, if invoked to bring money, and worldly manifestations, there would be no response. "All good things came to them who built up purity and strength of character." This alone was meant when Christ said, "But **seek first** his kingdom and his righteousness, and all these things will be given to you as well. Matthew 6:33" New International Version (NIV) If that is true, then it is equally true today.

Seeking the Kingdom does not mean faith in any existing religious group. It means to develop a condition of calmness or peace in the mind so that you may allow an inflow of Divine Wisdom, when one becomes in sync with the Supreme, he dwells in Heaven. "Heaven is within you." It's a condition of the mind and not a place. Income is the effect of the strength or weakness of one's character, which in turn was due to the manner of thinking and the nature of their thoughts.

With the Principle of Vibration and the Power of Imagination, anyone can make of themselves whatever they choose. Personality consists of the elements which have been named courage, confidence, judgment, decision, determination, aspiration, and truth. The degree in which they are possessed determines the power of the individual. The conditions of calmness and concentration allow the best use of these powers. Thoughts are vital, living, actual things, as real as Oxygen or Hydrogen. They come from without, and their value to any persons' mind depends on the condition of that mind. If the mind is strong and forceful it receives strong and forceful thoughts, which produce strength of character; if it is uninspiring and cowardly, it receives that class of thought which produces misery, poverty and poor health, and every thought received and issued from your mind make a stronger or weaker person of you.

The knowledge of these things does not produce results. But realization of this truth and watchfulness and control of your thoughts does. Ordinary individuals could barely believe that it is possible to attain higher powers by their minds. By lower plains of mind that conditions the attitude that would cause some to ridicule any new invention or idea in contrast to the promoter, who could clearly see the possibility of the project. It is the ability in one to see a truth when told of it, the lack of ability in the other to accept any portion of it.

These plains have existed since history began and have been the greatest hindrance of improving the world, particularly in regards to morals and religion. The lower attitudes being greater have obstructed the expression of thought of the lesser amounts of advanced thinkers. Galileo was compelled to retract his discovery of the Earth evolving around the Sun and the inquisition was instituted by the gross minded church men to limit freedom of thought.

"The Thief"

<u>*Be on the lookout for a thief who is working in your neighborhood.*</u> *It appears that no locks or home security systems are able to keep him from entering. He has been known to steal your health and energy and carry away your peace of mind and contentment. His name is* <u>*Depression.*</u>

He is no respecter of persons. He troubles men and women, young and old, rich and poor. The difficult thing about Depression is that he appears in seconds, even on days when most things are going well. He slips in as soon as there is a quiet moment - after a phone call, while driving in traffic, when you lay down to rest. He may not leave you alone permanently, but you can get him under control.

Be watchful and act as soon as you hear him coming.

"Keep a close watch on all you do and think. Stay true to what is right and God will bless you and use you to help others." 1 Timothy 4:16 Living Bible (TLB)

CHAPTER 3

Keep Your Own Counsel

THERE ARE THOSE who cannot believe that these universal principles exist in the natural world. Their minds are of a different frequency, pre-occupied with worldly matters. They are blind to spiritual truths and call others visionaries. If minds capable of half seeing, half belief in these things, is brought into contact with them it will be blinded by their blindness.

"God introduces himself to you at the level of the consciousness in which you can understand him."

Keep still, and work to develop strength, courage, power, force, push, and good will. You will become strong enough to stand on your own feet in spite of any and all.

If, however, there are those among our friends who need these truths for their own welfare and are capable of accepting them, by all means tell them; but do not cast pearls before swines, for they will turn and tear you down. Be not afraid; do your duty each instant.

Do it as well as you can. Hope and expect better things and your success is assured. Cast away all doubt. Even all the combined forces on Earth cannot stop the Supreme force of your Mind.

Some say I was born this way. I am always impatient, worrying, and anxious. I cannot change it. Yes, you probably were born that way, but you can change it unless you determine that you cannot and do not try. If you do not try, that settles it, no power from God or man can do anything for you when you assume that attitude.

When I was a child and found myself, a bit challenged I would say that, "I could not do it." My Father would say, "Lose those words from your vocabulary. It is all in your mind. Approach everything you set out to do with a positive attitude."

Your character, the will that compels you to be ignorant at one thing and pleased at another, has been formed as it now is by your parentage and the frame of thought that surrounded you. It constructed a motor, the subconscious on which one electrical current of life acts, while an equally strong current of different construction has no effect. A man is the product of his ancestors' thoughts and conditions. His present condition is the result of past thoughts. His future condition will be the result of his present thoughts.

"Two Commas"

Have you ever held a check in your hands with two commas? Instead of thinking about making a hundred thousand dollars a year, think about giving away a hundred thousand dollars. Write out a personal check to an organization or person that you would donate to, place it where you could see it daily, and feel the emotion that you would have when you deliver it. The emotion activates the vibration.

Your mind is not entirely in your body, but acts on your body and through the body, both consciously and subconsciously determines the status of the individual. By mind, I do not refer to the brain, which is truly a portion of the body, just as the nerves and muscles. Conscious mind is the intelligent recognition of self. Again, your mind is not your brain. Your mind surges through your brain, renews your tissues, and if it left your body your brain would still be in your body; nothing more than a senseless mass.

Passion in a person develops gradually through generations. A lot of the emotions that you have today were handed down from your ancestors through your parents. These emotions or states of mind were in the minds of people hundreds of years ago from their blood tree. The children unconsciously receive the thoughts and it becomes a part of them. If receptive he will grasp the qualities whether good or bad from his parents. If positive in his own individuality, he will not be harmed by the parent's characteristics. This explains why some children are so different from others in the same family. Your mind today is your ancestor's power of love, justice, confidence, determination, and those qualities which make up the personality. These qualities are either increased or diminished by the kinds of thoughts that you have during your life as an individual. These elements are not only received from people but also from the Divine.

Life which surrounds us fills the spirit in which we are composed of. They flow from one brave person to another, constantly strengthening them, and both are connected with the great bodies of these elements from which they receive a constant flow.

Two elements of the mind, Love and Intellect, constitute the whole mind of the person. To be successful you must bring all fear and its resulting emotions under the control of the will, or destroy them entirely, and to that end we devote our attention. When the mind is in condition of harmony, the emotions under the control of the will, it produces a condition of peace and allows the inflow of wisdom. An infinite wisdom which produces progression. It will carry one from poor health and poverty to health and sufficient income for all needs.

This is a law, a progression of success, and you are being deprived of just rights if you do not have every needful thing. It is natural for you to have money, friends, and happiness. Any other state of existence is unnatural. You have the right to enjoy life, follow the occupation you choose, do as you please so as long as what you please does not injure anyone, either in thought or action. This is your natural condition, and nothing but the action of your mind can deprive you of it. It is a law. Live in this law and your progress is speedy, your development is assured, and returns are in *Hard Cold Cash.*

Expect poverty and failure and you will get that. People think of you just as you think of yourself. One of my very first apartments that I lived in, as an adult, was in a neighborhood with a lakefront view. My friends would always tease me by saying, "that I was trying to act like a big-shot and should just save that extra rent money by living with them as a roommate in a less desirable neighborhood." They would say that they would never be able to afford a home in that area. I would reply, "As long as you think that you cannot, you are right." Most people defeat themselves in their minds before they ever invest any energy in the dream or task.

"If you consider yourself smart it is because you do not have enough wisdom to realize how little the wisest men or women know."

Joseph & Jennifer Gamboa

Thoughts:_____

"Change Freeways"

Some of us have Hi-powered minds that are limited to the pace of surrounding minds. It may be in the workplace, the local church, the sports bar, the barbershop, or even in our own home. We get complacent, comfortable, content, and eventually reduce the frequency of our true power.

If you have a high-performance vehicle, such as a Mercedes AMG, or Porsche Cayenne Turbo; regardless of the horse power underneath the hood, you are still limited to the speed of the traffic you are in.

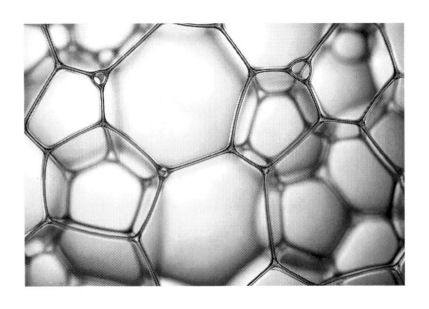

CHAPTER 4

It's All Mental

E VERYTHING IS BEING born, growing, dying, the very instant the thing reaches its height it begins to decline. The law of rhythm is in constant operation. Nothing is permanent but change. Everything seems to evolve from other things and resolves into other things. A constant action and reaction, building up and tearing down, creation and destruction, birth, growth and death, nothing endures but change. The All is unknowable. The All must be all there is; there is nothing existing outside of the All. Otherwise, the All would not be the All. There is nothing to confine or limit the All. It must be infinite in time or eternal. Nothing else could have created it. Something never evolves from nothing. If it had never "not been" even for a moment, it would not be now. It must continuously exist forever, for there is nothing to destroy it. It can never be undone even for a moment because something can never come from nothing. It must be infinite in space.

It must be everywhere for there is no place outside of the All. It cannot be otherwise, then continuous in space without break, separation or interruption for there is nothing to break, separate or interrupt its continuity. There is nothing which to fill in the gaps. It must be infinite in power, absolute for there is nothing to limit or restrict, restrain or confine, disturb or condition it. It is subject to no other power for there is no other power. We must begin with the understanding of the principle of the All. The All is mental. The All is Consciousness. There can be nothing that can change its real nature because there is nothing to change upon it and nothing which it could change. It cannot be added to or subtracted from. Increased or diminished. Nor become greater or lesser in any respect what so ever. It must have always been and always remain. The All is infinite and unchangeable. This reasoning must follow that anything finite and changeable cannot be the All.

Let's break that down. Everything we see around us is called matter, which is the physical foundation of all forms. Is the All merely matter? Not at all! Matter cannot make itself into life or consciousness. As life and consciousness are not made in the universe, thus the All cannot be matter. Science informs us that there really is no such thing as matter. For what we call matter is merely interrupted energy. Energy or force at a low rate of vibration. Even material science has abandoned the theory of matter. And now rest on the basis of energy. Then is the All energy or force?

Energy and force are blind. They are just mechanical things void of life or consciousness. Life or consciousness can never evolve from just blind energy or force. Nothing can rise higher than its source. Nothing evolved unless it is involved. The All cannot be mere energy or force, for if it were then there would be no such thing as life and consciousness in existence. What is higher than matter and energy? Life and consciousness and all their varying degrees are higher than matter and energy. A living conscious, that is as far above humans as the stars are above the lowest levels of the Earth. Spirit is beyond our understanding.

Joseph & Jennifer Gamboa

"The Apple Seed"

If I held an apple seed in my hand, what would you see, a seed or a tree? A Free Thinker would see 'An Apple Orchard.'

"The oak waits in the acorn, the bird sleeps in the egg. What is sleeping in you?"

"Bring out what is inside you, and this will save you; keep what is inside you and this will destroy you." Jesus 'The Book of Enoch'

Paracelsus wrote, "When a human undertakes to create something, he establishes a new heaven, as it were, and from it the work that he desires to create flows into him."

Patience comes from the Latin-*patiens* from *pati* which means; to suffer. Patience is a difficult characteristic to govern. But it is this vital patience or suffering that applies to the process of creation operating in humans. Whether it is coal to diamonds, water to ice, human spirit to divine, there must be suffering of purification and separation.

Humans know that the central task is the creation of oneself; and will pursue this task with great unbounded patience, "suffering." With this spiritual knowledge, evolution accomplished during long periods of time may be accomplished in a comparatively short time.

With this spiritual knowledge, evolution accomplished during long periods of time may be accomplished in a comparatively short time. However, the one who is attracted by material power will not obtain possession of this spiritual power.

What is the universe? We see that there can be nothing outside the All. Then is the universe the All? It must proceed in some way away from the All. It must be a creation of the All. But as something can never come from nothing, what can the source have used to create it? I cannot build a house without the dirt, the clay or without the wood. So where did the wood, the clay, the materials come from? Say that the All created the universe from itself, from the being or substance of itself. But then again, it cannot be subtracted or divided from as we have seen. So how is this so? If so, every particle of the universe would be aware of its being the All. The All cannot lose its knowledge of itself. Or actually become an atom or a blind force or low living thing.

The universe is our home and we will explore its farthest recesses before the end of time. We are dwelling in the infinite mind of the All. The possibilities and opportunities are infinite both in time and space. At the end of this grand cycle, when the All shall draw back into itself all of its creations, you will go gladly for you will then know the whole truth of being one with God. But in the meantime, rest calm and serene that you are safe and protected by the Infinite power.

Absolute truth has been defined as things in the mind of God, as God knows them. While relative truth is things as the relative human understands them. The higher we rise on the scale of consciousness, nearer to the mind of the Father, the more apparent the illusionary nature of finite things. We need not dwell upon illusions. Rather let us realize the real nature of the universe. Seek to understand the mental laws. The endeavors to use them at the best effect of our upward progress through life as we travel from plain to plain of being.

We may control matter. But we do so by controlling the higher forces. We may deny its mastery over us and rightly so but we should not attempt to ignore it in its relative aspect. At least as long as we dwell upon its plain. The laws of nature do not become less effective when we know them. Likewise, to be merely mental creations they are in full effect on various plains. We overcome the lower laws by applying higher ones and this is the journey. We must learn to apply higher laws. We cannot escape the laws that exist or rise above it. But we must learn how to apply them.

Higher Laws

I am attempting to express that the nature of the universe is mental. Thus, follow the example of the wise which the same authority states to use laws against the laws and the higher against the lower by the art of mental transformation. Remember always that transformation, not presumptuous denial, is the weapon of the master. Our business in the universe is not to deny his existence but to live using the laws to rise from lower to higher.

Emotional Intelligence

The Universe does not respond to your words. It responds to your vibrations. Your vibrations are a reflection of how you feel; therefore, the underlying impulse is from your emotions.

Your words are just a reflection of how you feel. It is your emotions that activate the vibrations on the wavelength. It is these vibrations that will influence what you attract. Be careful what you say, for that may trigger how you feel. The real power comes from the feelings.

Everything is in God. It is equally true that God is in everything. The spirit of my creator is inherent within me, and yet I am not he! This basically means that if a painter formed an image or an ideal in his head in which to express his art, the image that appears in the art is not the creator.

He may have some of the attributes of the painter because the painter created him in his mind to express a certain kind of personality. The painter is actually in the image of what he has painted. But it is foolish for the image to come alive and think that he is the painter.

Another example of this is the characters in Shakespeare such as Hamlet or Othello or Richard 3rd. You can see all of Shakespeare in these characters, he imparted all of his personality and creativity into these characters but Othello cannot come out one day and say, "I am Shakespeare." That makes the same sense as man saying, "I am God". God may have designed us to have unique and individual personality but we cannot claim to be the Creator. The spirit of the Creator is inherent within us and yet we are not the Creator. The All is in the earthworm and yet the earthworm is far from being the All. Yet the wonder remains though the earthworm exists merely as a lowly thing created and having its being solely within the mind of the All. The All is imminent in the earthworm and in the particle, that goes to make up the earthworm. In the degree that the human being realizes the existence of the spirit dwelling deep within the self; will rise in the spiritual scale of life? This is what spiritual development means, the recognition, realization, and manifestation of the spirit within us.

"The Mind Barrier"

In 1903, the mile record is 4 minutes 12.75 seconds. This record will never be broken. There was a fierce intellectual debate that the human body had reached its full potential. Proof was offered — because of the length of bones, the nature of muscles, and the construction of joints, it was proven that a human being could not run a mile any faster than 4 minutes and 12 and three quarters seconds.

In 1954, Roger Banister became the first person to break the 4-minute mile barrier. He opened the flood gates and his record was broken just a few weeks later. And the next year, a phenomenal 236 people also did what was considered impossible! Many athletes have broken the 4-minute barrier hundreds of times. Virtually every international 1500m/mile runner can get under 4 minutes.

The mind makes it possible.

Notes:_____

_____

_____

_____

_____

_____

_____

_____

_____

_____

_____

_____

_____

_____

_____

_____

_____

_____

_____

_____

_____

_____

_____

_____

_____

_____

_____

_____

_____

_____

_____

_____

_____

CHAPTER 5

The Fire Inside

THE MEANING OF spirit can be referred to as living power, animated force or inner essence. Those who obtain high spiritual powers and misuse them have a terrible fate in store for them. The swing of the pendulum of rhythm will eventually swing them back to the furthest extreme of material existence. Back to the point where they must retrace their steps spirit-ward, along the weary realms of the path. Unfortunately, on this return path it will always be with the added torture of having with them a lingering memory from which they fell, due to their evil actions. The striving for selfish power on spiritual plains eventually results in the spiritual soul losing its spiritual balance and falling back as far as it had previously risen. The legend of fallen angels is an example. But to even such a soul, the opportunity of a return is given, and each soul or such a soul can make the return journey.

In the Principle of Vibration, the positive pole seems to be of a higher degree than the negative pole, and readily dominates it. This is due to the tendency of nature which is in the direction of the dominant activity of the positive pole.

"Nothing rests; everything moves; everything vibrates; "everything". The difference of power is due entirely to the varying rates and mode of vibrations. Even God manifests a constant vibration of such an infinite degree of intensity and rapid motion that it can practically be considered at rest. Imagine the spirits at one end of the pole of vibration and the other pole, the opposite pole being physical extreme forms of matter. The lower the vibration the more matter. Between these two poles are millions upon millions of different rates and modes of vibration. Modern science has proven that, "all that we call matter and energy are but; modes of vibratory motions".

For instance, there is no such thing as cold; it is just an absence of heat. The difference is in the vibration of molecules or the speed the motion. The more absent the heat, the slower the vibratory modes and the more mass it possesses; just like water into ice. The more heat, the more the molecules expand which creates more motion in the molecules. Below 32 degrees Fahrenheit, water freezes and changes from a liquid to a solid. At 212 degrees, water becomes a gas, steam or almost invisible. This is all the result of a change in the vibrations, or motion of the molecules. When heat is applied, the molecules speed up. When the temperature is lowered, the molecules slow down.

"Serve"

How many times a day do you say the word, "Thank you?" How many times do you hear the word, "Thank you?" What is the difference? Serve my friends…

This applies to our minds from a negative state to a positive state. It is the level of degree of vibration and which end of the pole or spectrum are we thinking on?

Particles of matter are in a circular motion, from atoms to planets that revolve around the suns and the suns revolve around the galaxies. Molecules are composed of atoms and they are in a constant movement and vibration. Atoms are composed of electrons, protons, and ions which are also in a state of motion revolving around each other which manifest at a very rapid state and mode of vibration. The point is in vibrating. The nature of these phenomena is known as cohesion, which is basically the law of attraction. This is the principle of attraction in which every particle of mass or matter is bond to every other particle of mass. I will use the following illustration to show the effects of increasing rates of vibration.

Picture a wheel, a top or revolving cylinder, running at a low rate of speed. Let us suppose the object is moving slowly. It may be seen but no sound of its movement reaches the ear. The speed is gradually increased. In a few moments, its movement becomes so rapid that a deep growl or low note may be heard. Then as the rate is increased the note raises one notch in the musical scale. Then the motion being still further increased, the next highest note is now distinguished. Then one after another, all the notes of the musical scale appear, rising higher and higher as the motion is increased. Finally, when the motions have reached a certain rate the final note perceptible to human ears is reached and the shrill, piercing shriek dies away, silence follows. No sound is heard from the revolving object, the rate of motion being so high that the human ear cannot register the vibrations. Then the perception of heat follows. Then after quite some time the eye catches a glimpse of the object becoming a dull dark reddish color. As the rate increases, the red becomes brighter. Then as the speed is increased, the red melts into an orange. Then the orange melts into a yellow. The shades of green, blue, indigo, and finally violet, follow as the rate of speed increases. Then the violet fades away, and all color disappears, the human eye is not able to register them. But there are invisible rays emanating from the revolving object, the rays that are used in photographing, and other subtle rays of light. Then begin to manifest the peculiar rays known as the "X Rays," etc., as the constitution of the object changes. Electricity and Magnetism are emitted when the appropriate rate of vibration is attained.

When the object reaches a certain rate of vibration its molecules disintegrate, and resolve themselves into the original elements or atoms. Then the atoms, following the Principles of Vibration, are separated into the countless particles of which they are composed. Eventually, even the particles disappear and the object may be said to be composed of The Ethereal Substance. Science does not dare to follow the illustration further, but this teaches that if the vibrations can be continually increased the object would mount up the successive states of manifestation and would in turn manifest the various mental stages, and then on Spirit-ward, until it would finally re-enter the ALL, which is Absolute Spirit. The "object", however, would have ceased to be an "object" long before the stage of Ethereal Substance was reached, but otherwise the illustration is correct, in as much as it shows the effect of constantly increased rates and modes of vibration. It must be remembered, in the above illustration, that at the stages at which the "object" throws off vibrations of light, heat, etc., it is not actually "resolved" into those forms of energy (which are much higher in the scale), but simply that it reaches a degree of vibration in which those forms of energy are liberated, in a degree, from the confining influences of its molecules, atoms and particles, as the case may be. These forms of energy, although much higher in the scale than matter, are imprisoned and confined in the material combinations, by reason of the energies manifesting through, and using material forms, but thus becoming entangled and confined in their creations of material forms, which, to an extent, is true of all creations, the creating force becoming involved in its creation.

These teachings go much further than do those of modern science. They teach that all manifestation of thought, emotion, reason, will or desire, or any mental state or condition, are accompanied by vibrations, a portion of which are thrown off and which tend to affect the minds of other persons by "induction". This is the principle which produces the phenomena of "telepathy"; mental influence, and other forms of the action and power of mind over mind, with which the general public is rapidly becoming acquainted.

Every thought, emotion or mental state has its corresponding rate and mode of vibration. By an effort of the will of the person, or of the other persons, these mental states may be reproduced, just as a musical tone may be reproduced by causing an instrument to vibrate at a certain rate – just as color may be reproduced in the same way. By knowledge of the Principle of Vibration, as applied to Mental Phenomena, one may polarize the mind at any degree wished, thus gaining a perfect control over the mental states, moods, etc.

In the same way, a person may affect the minds of others, producing the desired mental states in them. In short, humans may be able to produce on the Mental Plain that which science produces on the Physical Plain – namely, "Vibrations at Will." This power of course may be acquired only by the proper instruction, exercise, and practice, etc., the science being that of Mind Transformation.

A little reflection on what we have said will show the student that the Principle of Vibration underlies the wonderful phenomena of the power manifested by the Masters and Adepts, who are able to apparently set aside the Laws of Nature, but in reality, are simply using one law against another; one principle against another principle, to accomplish their results by changing the vibrations of material objects, or forms of energy, and thus perform what are commonly called 'miracles.'

"The Fire Inside"

Once the fire inside me would burn like the California Sierra. With the belief that I was invincible, I could stop bullets. Suddenly, life snuffed it out! The raging furnace had been reduced to the flickering flame of a small candle; with the wind blowing. Then silently, alone, in the wee hours of the night, the flame went out.

Like a genie on a flying carpet, Grace flew in on a gentle breeze. Enough breath to resurrect the flame inside. Now fire trucks are powerless. "Even a half lit, lipstick-stained cigarette butt can burn down a forest."

CHAPTER 6

The Hindu Scorpion

E VERYTHING HAS POLES, everything has a pair of opposites; like and unlike are the same, and opposites are identical in nature but different in degree. Spirit and matter are just opposites of the same thing, one end of the pole to the other end of the pole. The only difference is the degrees of vibration. There is no such thing as cold, just the absence of heat. Heat and cold are identical in nature. They are just temperature which have differences in the degrees. There is no place on a thermometer where heat ceases and cold begins. It is all a matter of higher vibrations. If you travel far enough south you will eventually go north. Just as if you travelled far enough East you will end up West.

Like temperature, good and bad are not absolute. If you call one end of the scale good and the other bad, a thing is "less good" than a thing higher on the scale; but that "less good" thing is "more good" than a thing next below it, and so on and so on, this being regulated by a position on the scale. We can even apply this polarity between love and hate because there is no such thing as absolute love and absolute hate. The two are merely terms applied to the two poles of the same thing. As we ascend the scale we find more love and less hate. If we go down the scale we find more hate and less love. This is true no matter from what point, high or low, we may start on the scale. Fear and courage are on the same principle. Understanding this principle of polarity enables you to transform from one mental state to another.

On the other hand, on the lines of polarity, things that belong to different classes cannot be transformed into each other. Only things on the same class maybe changed. They can only have their polarity changed. For example, love never becomes north or south. However, hate may be transformed into love by changing its polarity. Courage may be transformed into fear by changing its polarity. Hard things may be rendered soft. Dull things may become sharp. Hot things become cold, if you change its polarity. Transformation has to always be between things of the same kind, just of different degrees.

Let's use an example of a fearful man. By raising his mental vibrations along the line of fear – courage, he can be filled with the highest degree of courage and fearlessness. The mental states belong to countless amounts of classes, and each class in which has opposite poles along which transformation is possible. Fear cannot be transformed into love nor can courage be transformed into hate.

You can change the polarity of your own mind or the level of vibration by the operation of this art of polarization. We may extend this beyond our own state of mind through the phenomena of mental influence. We see that mental influence is possible. The mental states may be produced by or from others. We can see how a certain rate of vibration of a certain mental state may be communicated to another person and his/her polarity; if that class of mental states has changed. For instance, a soldier in battle may be afraid and then a lieutenant may come along and by bringing his own mind up to the desired vibration by his trained will, and obtaining that desired vibration, he will produce a similar mental state in that of his fellow soldier. The result being that the vibrations are raised and the person polarizes toward the positive end of the scale instead of toward the negative. His fear and other negative emotions are transformed to courage and similar positive mental states. You will see that these states are matters of degree, and you will be able to raise or lower the vibration at will, to change your mind, and become the master of your state of mind, instead of being the servant or slave.

"The Nature of You"

There was this Hindu who saw a scorpion floundering around in the water. He decided to save it by stretching out his finger, but the scorpion stung him. The man still tried to get the scorpion out of the water, but the scorpion stung him again.

A man nearby told him to stop saving the scorpion that kept stinging him.

But the Hindu said: "It is the nature of the scorpion to sting. It is my nature to love. Why should I give up my nature to love just because it is the nature of the scorpion to sting?"

CHAPTER 7

The Tides of Life

E VERYTHING FLOWS IN and out. All things rise and fall and then rise again. The pendulum swing manifests in everything. The measure of the swing to the right is the measure of the swing to the left. Rhythm compensates. The principle of rhythm is closely related to the principle of polarity. There is always an action and reaction; an advance and a retreat; a rising and a sinking; in the entire universe. Suns, worlds, humans, animals, plants, minerals, forces, energy, mind, and even spirit manifest this principle, in the rise and fall of nations, in the life history of all things, and even in the mental states of the human being. Things are born and grow old and die only to be reborn. Night always follows day; and day always follows night. The pendulum swings from summer to winter and then back again. All atoms and molecules swing around the circle of their nature. There is no such thing as absolute rest, no such thing as cessation from movement, and all movement has rhythm.

There is always the rhythmic swing from one pole to the other. The universal pendulum is ever in motion. The tides of life flow in and out according to this divine law. This universal influence extends to the mind of man, and it accounts for continued mood swings, feelings, and other perplexing changes we notice in our behavior. But understanding this principle you will have learned how to escape some of the activities of this pendulum swing by mind transformation.

There are two great plains of consciousness, the lower plains and the higher plain. By understanding this fact, you can rise to the higher plain and can escape the swing of the rhythmic pendulum which manifests on the lower plain. In other words, if the swing of the pendulum occurred on the unconscious plain, the consciousness would not affect it. This is called the law of neutralization. It consists of raising the ego above vibrations of the plain of mental activity, so that the negative swing of the pendulum does not manifest in consciousness and therefore are not affected. It's like rising above something beneath you. If one refuses to participate in a backward swing of the pendulum it will deny its influence over the person and stands firm in the polarized position, and this will allow the mental pendulum to swing back along the unconscious plain. By applying the law of neutralization, we refuse to allow our moods and negative mental states to affect us. By continued practice we can obtain a degree of poise and mental firmness almost impossible of the belief on the part of those who allow themselves to be swung backward and forward by the mental pendulum of moods and feelings.

The majority of people have very little control over their feelings. If you stop for a moment and consider, you would think about how many swings of rhythm have affected you and your life. How a period of enthusiasm has been followed by an opposite feeling of melancholy? Like a mood or period of courage has been followed by an equal mood of fear. The tides of feelings of people rise and fall, but they never suspect the cause or the reason for this mental phenomenon. If we take time to contemplate and understand this principle, it will give us the keys to understand the rhythmic swings of these feelings and allow us to better avoid being carried away by these inflows and outflows of tides. The will is superior to the conscious manifestation of this principle, although the principle itself can never be destroyed. It may escape its effects, but the principle operates never the less.

"Following the principle of rhythm brings us to the law of compensation. Compensation is to counter balance. "The measure of the swing to the right is the measure to the swing to the left; the law of compensation is that the swing in one direction determines the swing in the opposite direction. One balances or counter balances the other. The pendulum of the clock swings a certain distance to the right and then an equal distance to the left. The seasons balance each other the same way. The tides follow the same law. An object hurled up in the sky to a certain height has an equal distance to fall and return to the Earth. This law of compensation and counter balance applies to the mental states as well.

The person, who enjoys too much, is subject to suffer a lot, while the person who feels very little pain is capable of feeling very little joy. The rule is the capacity for pain and pleasure, in each individual, are balanced. An example of this is the person that is immune to discipline is also immune to gratitude and enjoying things. Not necessarily immune but a low sensation of this emotion and the same sensation of the opposite. One who does not feel the great depths of sadness because of the limits of the range of their heart cannot feel the great rises of joy because of the limitations in the heart and the mental ability restricts them. Before one can enjoy a certain degree of pleasure they must have swung as far, proportionately, toward the other pole or feeling. This by no means is to say that experiencing a certain degree of pleasure will not be followed by a certain degree of pain.

By an advanced transformation of mind, one can escape the swing toward pain by the process of neutralization mentioned earlier. By rising to the higher plain of the ego much of the experience of those dwelling on the lower plain is avoided and escaped. Everything has its pleasant and unpleasant sides. Things that one gains are always paid for by things that one loses. The rich possess much that the poor lack while the poor often possess things that are beyond the reach of the rich. The millionaire may have the desire to feast while he lacks the appetite to enjoy it; they envy the appetite of the laborer, who lacks the wealth of the millionaire but gets more pleasure from the common food than the millionaire could ever obtain.

"In Your Hands"

A student who was angry with his teacher for a failing grade decided to embarrass the teacher in public. The student had a small bird in his hand and he asked the teacher if it was alive or dead. Regardless of what the teacher would say, the student planned to prove him wrong by crushing the bird or setting it free. When he asked the question the teacher replied, "The life you are holding is in your hands."

SECTION 2

CHAPTER 8

The Determined Mind

THE PERSON WHO is confident, determined and maintains a strong mental attitude is not likely to be affected by negative thoughts of discouragement and failure coming from the minds of others. At the same time if these negative thoughts reach someone who is pitched on a low keynote or frequency they will deepen his negative state and add fuel to the fire which is consuming his strength, or smother the fire of his energy and activity.

Determination is usually confused with stubbornness and a dominating desire to rough ride over everyone who has opposing ideas; the desire to bulldoze and overpower without regard to right or wrong. This kind of individual is self-willed and will not be moved by reason, logic, and superior wisdom. You know the people, who have it all figured out?" You can't tell them anything but they can continually suggest what you should do. They will sacrifice friends, money, and family to have their own way. This attitude of mind is one of ignorance, intense selfishness, and one in which determination has no part. It is usually brought about by circumstances controlling the individual, and by the individual living under circumstances which produce a narrow frame of mind and therefore, a narrow life. Studying something new, traveling and engaging with others from all classes of life can assist in taking most of these characteristics away.

The determined mind does not rush along, does not try to force things, but is content to wait if waiting will bring results. It makes friends, avoids obstacles, but never loses sight of its purpose. The determined mind calculates, reasons, seeks ideas, use ideas which seem better than its own, and finally lays its plans and cannot be diverted from its purpose.

You can develop this quality by thinking of staying persistent and focused on one goal and purpose; by not allowing others to determine what you will do; by not giving up when obstacles get in the way; and by repeating the words mentally and verbally; "I am determined; I am powerful; I will succeed;" until this quality is imprinted in the subconscious mind and it becomes a part of your personality. This will carve out a look of determination upon your face for the body expresses just what the mind holds.

Atmosphere

Do not associate with negative energy minded individuals. If you are the daughter or son, husband or wife, stay away from their discouraging ways for they are like poison. Blood ties give it no law for them to destroy you one word at a time.

Seek a more positive circle. Sometimes we believe our family and friends are what is best for us. Most of the time this is the case; but often, our ambitions and goals will be chained at the link of their ambitions and goals without us realizing it. Of course, they will always love us, but you have to get down to business and get after your pursuit for what the Divine Inspiration has inspired you to do. Sometimes this requires a higher level of mental energy in your atmosphere to grow. Look at it like this. If I plant tomato seeds in a small nursery pot, after several weeks of the fermenting it will break the soil. If I keep all the seeds together in that confined space, (atmosphere), it is only a matter of time before they all occupy the entire space, therefore limiting and indefinitely restricting all further growth; however, if I remove a seed or two to the garden outside, the tomatoes will have access to stretch in all directions for their naturally inspired development.

Before you leave the garden, continue to be polite and reflect a positive nature, and make hopeful suggestions, sowing the seed in the minds of those you leave behind (mentally). Do not sit down to see it grow. Keep it moving. Never feel that it is your duty to stay close and monitor the atmosphere of despair.

If so, then you might as well think that it is your duty to stay in deep water with someone who does not want to put in the effort to swim. Swim for the shore and throw out a line, but do not remain in those waters until you are dragged under.

If you find anyone determined to talk failure, sickness, and misfortune; and find very little else to talk about, walk away. Would you allow someone who was very dear to you to slowly poison you if you knew it? Then why would you think it is your duty to take doses of despondency which paralyze your ambitions? Despondency is an insult to the Creator. You do not have to justify keeping those people at bay who give you less hope than when you met them. Do not associate with them intimately until they learn how to speak hopefully and more positive thoughts. The exchange of energy is very important.

CHAPTER 9

A Living Sun

T HOUGHTS ARE CARRIED along like a leaf by the wind, obedient to environment and outside forces, moods, and desires. Never mind the desires and wills of others whose thoughts are stronger than themselves, and the power of suggestion carrying them along without resistance on their part. Leaves flow like thoughts. Even the trees possess the intelligence when to cry by shedding their leaves to prepare for a new season.

Moved like the pawns on the chess board of life, they play their parts and are laid aside after the game is over. Then there are those, knowing the rules of the game, who rise up above the plain of the material life and place themselves in touch with the higher powers of their nature, they dominate their own moods, qualities, and polarity as well as the environment around them. They become movers in the game instead of pawns, and causes instead of effects. They do not escape the cause of the higher plains but fall in with the higher laws, and thus master circumstances on the lower plain. They form a conscious part of the law instead of being mere blind instruments. While they serve on the higher plains, they rule on the material plain.

"The Empty Space"

You can buy a house, but you can't buy a home. You can buy sex, but you can't buy love. You can buy a car, but you can't buy safety.

Can you grab sunlight and put it in your pocket? The glass may hold the wine, but it's the empty space that fills the glass. The four walls provide the house, but it's the empty space that we dwell in. Pay attention to this space. This is your space. Come in harmony with it. Make peace with it, and it will serve you.

We are able to see clearly that everything is governed by universal law; that the numbers of laws are but manifestations of the one great law, the law which is the All. Indeed, not even a sparrow flies unnoticed by the consciousness of God, there is nothing outside of law, nothing. Man may use law to overcome laws and the higher will always prevail against the lower, until at least he has reached the stage in which he seeks refuge in the law itself.

Knowledge like wealth is intended for use. Knowledge without use is an expression of a vain thing bringing no good to its possessor and others. Be aware of knowledge in action and express into action that which you have learned.

The evolving spirit must realize that it has everything it requires. It may suggest advice and bits of knowledge as it goes along, the soul being its own judge, but in the end, it must do its own work. All teachings in the world will not help you unless you take hold of the matter yourself and work out your own salvation. You cannot get true mental or spiritual teaching by simply paying so much for a course of lessons and doing nothing yourself. You must bring something to the table before you can take anything away. You must work up to an understanding before the teachings of another will do you any good. The teacher may open up a suggestion that will open up a line of thought for you, or he may point out a way that has proven value to him; and thus, save you much time and trouble. In the end, you must do the real work yourself.

A teacher may be so filled with the truth that he will overflow, and you will get some of the overflow. I believe that this truth is "catching". But even so, unless you make that truth your own by living it out loud, and applying it to your needs, it will do you no good.

As long as you are content to "sit at his feet," you will not grow one inch. You will be merely a reflection of the teacher instead of being an individual.

We need a reminder of this point once in a while. It is so easy to have your thoughts predigested for you by some teacher or writer, so easy to receive your teachings in bits. It is easy to sit down and digest the tabloid that the teacher or writer has kindly prepared for you, and imagine that you are getting the real thing. But I tell you friends, it won't do the work. Take all the teachings that you please, but you have to get down to business yourself. You can't give someone else power of attorney to do the work in your place. Life accepts no substitutes, you must step up yourself. It is extremely easy; this idea of paying so much, in time or money, to some teacher or lesson, and then sneaking into the Kingdom of Heaven, holding on to his or her robe; but it won't work. You have to do some hustling on your own account, and don't make any mistake about this fact.

I look around at many people around me "sitting at the feet" of someone, sinking their individuality in that of the teacher, and not daring to think of the original thought, never mind should it conflict with the notion of the teacher. These good souls are so full of the teachings that they can repeat them, phrase by phrase, like a well-trained parrot. But they don't understand a bit of it. They are like the moon which shines by reason of the reflection of the sun's rays, and has no light or heat of its own. The talk of these "disciples" and "sitters-at-the-feet" is nothing but moonshine, mere reflected light.

Moons are dead, cold things, no light, no heat, no fire, and no energy. Dead cold, barren and "played out." Stop this moon business and build yourself up into a Sun. You have it in you, manifest it. Start yourself in motion and manifest Life. You don't have to solve all the riddles of the Universe before you can do something. Just get down to the task that lies ahead of you, and throw into it some of that Great Life Principle that is within you waiting for a chance to manifest itself. No person has a monopoly of knowing or a corner of the market on the truth. It is accessible to you as much as anyone else, but you must dig for it. Stop being moons. Stop living by reflected light. Get into the Sun. Carry out into the Sun the teachings that are offered you, and see whether or not they fade. Apply the chemical of laughter and see whether it bleaches. Get into the action and convert yourself into a Living Sun. You can do it! It is within your power. Every human soul contains within it the elements of the Sun, get to work and express yourself.

"Evolve"

Albert Einstein once said, "No problem can be solved from the level of consciousness that created it."

One of Early Man's first problems was the night. He became tired of being a late-night snack on the menu of lions and hyenas on the Okavango Delta. He had to evolve his way of thinking to overcome this constant challenge. He learned to control fire. This gave him protection, warmth, and light. With less fear in the night, he had access to new ways of creating and thinking. He could walk further to explore his world; in which of course, he would find ice glaciers. This constituted a whole new set of problems. I had a problem one night when I could not find a Jack-in-the Box on Ocean Blvd. You get the point.

Any demand made upon man creates a new idea. Unemployment in a bad economy can shut us down, or allow us an opportunity to evolve to the next level to overcome our dilemma. Some go from working on the plant floor at GM to starting their own Auto repair business. New life conditions create new ways of thinking, which create new life conditions.

"Knowledge is knowing the facts; Wisdom is knowing what to do with the facts" B.J Palmer

Joseph & Jennifer Gamboa

Thoughts:_____

_____
_____
_____
_____
_____
_____
_____
_____
_____
_____
_____
_____
_____
_____
_____
_____
_____
_____
_____
_____
_____
_____
_____
_____
_____
_____
_____
_____
_____
_____
_____

CHAPTER 10

Natural Intelligence Applications & Exercises

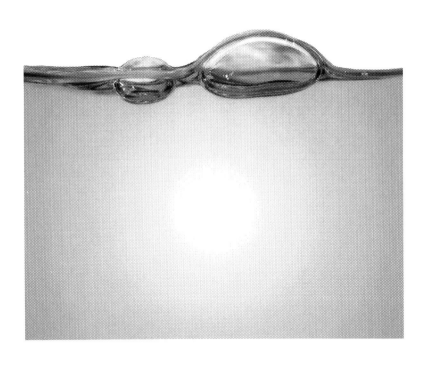

<u>1: Breath *(Spirit)*</u>

W HEN I was in the United States Marine Corps Boot Camp, Parris Island, South Carolina, I was astonished with how many things we had to learn before ever touching a weapon. One of the first parts of training was learning how to save lives, rather than taking them. "Start the breathing, stop the bleeding, protect the wound, and treat for shock." It suddenly dawned on me the significance of breath. It is the first thing we do and it is the last thing we do. It is the essential entrance and the exit for human life.

As stated early in the book, 'breath' is from the Latin word, 'Spiritus.' Therefore, our breathing has a direct influence on our spirit. Heart attacks, cancer, strokes, pneumonia, asthma, speech problems, and almost every disease known to mankind is worsened or improved by how well we breathe.

The average person reaches peak respiratory function and lung capacity in their mid-20's. Then they begin to lose respiratory capacity: between 9% and 25% for every decade of life! So, unless you are doing something to maintain or improve your breathing capacity, it will decline, and with it, your general health, your life expectancy, and for that matter, your spirit too!

Given an optimal diet, the respiratory system should be responsible for eliminating 70% of your metabolic waste? The remainder should be eliminated through defecation 3%, urination 8%, and perspiration 19%. So, if you think that going to the bathroom every day is important, or that working up a good sweat now and then is healthy, think again about the value of full free optimal breathing!

According to several European medical doctors and numerous Taoist, Buddhist, Hindu, Hawaiian, and Native American healers and spiritual teachers, there are at least 200 conditions of life and diseases that relate directly to incorrect breathing. America's own Dr. Andrew Weil states that "Improper breathing is a common cause of ill health. The human body needs continuous supply of energy to keep the basic living characteristics in place. This energy is obtained through oxidation. For oxidation, oxygen is required. If there is no supply of oxygen, meaningful oxidation would stop, thus energy supply would stop, resulting in the death of the human body.

Exercise 1

Turn off anything that is emitting an electrical frequency, such as a cell phone, television, computer, etc. Remove your shoes and sit comfortably in a chair with your feet flat on the floor, this will ground you, in a relaxed position.

Take **5** slow and deep breaths through your nostrils only. Breathe from your diaphragm. Picture that when you inhale, that you are inhaling pure white light. Imagine dark smoke blowing out of your nostrils when you exhale. This will remove toxins from you spirit.

Next, make a fist with your right hand. Extend your thumb and your pinky finger. It may kind of look like a gang sign. Place your thumb over your right nostril so that no air can come in or out. Breathe in the left open nostril for **4 seconds**. Now close the left nostril with the pinky finger, simultaneously pinching both nostrils close.

Hold your breath and the white light in, for **8 seconds.** Next, release your thumb from your right nostril, still holding the left nostril close, exhale from your right nostril for **6 seconds.**

Now breathe in the open right nostril for **4 seconds.** Close the right nostril with your thumb. Hold your breath and the white light in, for **8 seconds.** Release the pinky finger from your left nostril and exhale for **6 seconds.** Again, inhale through left nostril for **4 seconds** and close. Repeat this cycle for a total of five minutes. You may gradually increase the time as this will develop your oxidation.

You are gradually accumulating carbon dioxide in the body. The deep breaths restore the oxygen content of the blood and remove enough carbon dioxide to allow the breath to be held longer and therefore more carbon dioxide to be produced. The carbon dioxide makes the chemical balance of the blood more acidic, and it slows the activity of the nerves and the brain.

The Sun has a powerful magnetic field; therefore, when doing this exercise; it is better to face the East in the mornings and the West in the evenings. This daily breathing application will balance and activate your spirit. Picture a sealed glass jar with baby powder resting on the bottom. If you were to hold and shake the jar, the powder will touch all the space within the bottle. This exercise will shake lose all of the settled spirit from your molecules and assimilate your spirit in proper balance throughout your entire body and mind.

2: Water *(Elevation)*

Water is the medium in which all nature is governed. It takes up 74% of the planet, yet we are completely ignorant to its intelligence. The human body, depending on age, consists of 70-90% water. The brain is made up of 85% water. 1.5 liters per day is absorbed through our skin as we bathe or shower. Why is this important when water is just water?

The chemical composition of water is the same throughout, but the significance is in the structure of the water. The structure is how its molecules are organized. There is a divine spark imprinted in water. It has memory. Its molecules are organized into clusters, each cluster having memory cells. There are 440,000 information panels in each memory cell.

It is directly influenced by positive and negative human emotions. Why are we baptized in water? Why do we pray for our food? Water is endowed with a self-cleansing capacity. Science has measured the frequency of prayer, which is 8 hertz in any language. This corresponds with the oscillation of the Earth's magnetic field, which is also 8 hertz. When we pray we are not only blessing the food, but physically altering the properties of the water locked in the food.

In nature water always takes a smooth and natural course. By the time it reaches our home it has taken a series of 90-degree angles through pipes in our supply systems, is chemically treated, and becomes deformed. In fact, if you placed identical bowls in front of any animal or pet it will always chose water from a spring loaded with natural energies. We pollute water spiritually and it absorbs the energy in a home, whether positive or negative.

For any process to begin requires an impulse. The following exercise will teach you how to elevate water.

Exercise 2

Locate a retail store or market and purchase a small glass container with a lid. You can generally find this in a kitchenware section. It is important to have a new container for this application, for it has no residue or energy that may inhibit the process. If for some reason you do not live next to a natural spring or glacier, purchase a 32oz or 1 liter of natural spring water that is distributed directly from the source.

Tape a small photo of someone or something that brings you joy each time you lay your eyes on it. It may be a photo of your children, when they were still innocent of course, or your cat or dog, or anything else that stimulates a positive emotion from you.

Fill the container with the natural spring water. Next, place the container outside, or indoors on a window ledge where it can absorb the maximum amount of the sun. You may have to place it facing the East in the mornings and West in the evenings. In the evening, if you can view the moon, place the water in that direction. Why? Every day the moon dances with the oceans. It is a powerful partnership formed by gravity. Your water will experience its effects.

After you have done this for a day or two, place a set of headphones around the container, plugged into your music source. Now play some classical music, preferably concerto, string instruments such as the violin, or even piano. "Antonia Vivaldi, *The Four Seasons*," is an excellent choice for delivering a harmonious frequency. Do this for about an hour.

Next, in the most comfortable place in your home, hold the container in both hands, look at the photo and say aloud, "thank you, thank you, thank you." "I love you, I love you, I love you."

82

Pray. Say it as many times as you like before you convince yourself that you are doing something silly. Human emotion has the most powerful influence on water. The most intelligent and powerful emotions are **Love and Gratitude.**

Now you have activated and elevated the water. If you were to look at it under a microscope the structure of the molecules would be well organized and harmonious and thousands of times more active. You can use it in any manner you desire. 10 grams of elevated water diluted in 60 liters of regular water will change all the entire 60 liters to the structure and energetic properties of the elevated water.

You may pour some into your coffee, tea, orange juice, pet bowl, or even your bottled water. It will immediately restore the buoyancy, PH levels, and the electromagnetic charge in your blood cells.

3: Center *(Concentration)*

Concentration is a condition of the mind that may be developed through the individual mind. This state of mind is an essential quality for success. A perfect state of concentrative power will allow you to give the whole force of the intellect to whatever you may be doing at each particular moment. This will enable you to do whatever task at hand better and continually adds to the power for you developing your mind. By holding the thought of concentration and by building it up, your strength of mind and force of personality will constantly be increased.

Every family has a thought atmosphere which forms a mental lake and whoever comes into contact with this atmosphere can feel the influence of this thought energy upon them. Have you ever been in someone's home where you felt uncomfortable and had to get-away? This is because you felt the thought atmosphere or mental lake of that family, and it was not as peaceful as your own state of mind.

In business when a man or a woman has the power to give his or her whole mind to a particular idea, which he or she is entertaining at that moment, he or she will adjust it, assimilate it, and pick out the true and reject the false, and will benefit through that wisdom, which is from the power of concentration. The lack or underdevelopment of this quality produces more of a scattered brain man or woman, and their thoughts run from here and there uselessly exhausting their mentality.

Nervousness is the lack of concentration. In fact, half of the bodies illness is from throwing unconstructive thoughts around at random, for the body is just an expression of the mind. By holding your thoughts to one thing at a time, then changing the character by consciousness of the will, putting no more power into each thought than necessary to its successful conclusion, enables the mind to constantly gather strength. The body will soon follow by becoming more vigorous, elastic, buoyant, and healthy. Once started on this line your mind will lead you on and show you the way. The concentrative mind is the mind of power.

The first requisite for concentrating is the ability to shut out outside sounds, thoughts, and sights; to obtain perfect control of mind and body. The body must be brought under the direct control of the mind and the mind under the direct control of the will. The will is strong enough but the mind needs strengthening by being brought under the direct influence of the will. The mind, strengthened by the impulse of the will, becomes a much more powerful projector of thought vibrations, than otherwise, and the vibrations have much greater force and effect.

Exercise 3: Con-Centering

Involuntary Concentration

This may seem simple, but it is a very effective conditioning exercise for developing your ability to focus. Sit erect in a comfortable chair, with your head up and your chin out, and your shoulders thrown back. Raise your right arm until it is level with your shoulder, pointing to the right. The palm of your hand should be turned downward. Turn your head and stare at your fingertips, keeping your arm perfectly steady for one minute. Repeat with the left arm. Increase the time by one minute each day, until you are able to maintain this position for five minutes.

Fill a wine glass full of water, and taking the glass between the fingers, extend the right arm directly in front of you. Fix your eyes on the glass and attempt to hold it so steady so that you will not notice any movement of the water. Do this exercise for one minute and increase by one minute each day until five minutes is reached. Alternate with the left arm.

Voluntary Concentration

Sit in front of a table, placing your hands on the table, your fists clinched with the back of your hands lying on the table, palms facing up. Wrap the thumb around the fingers. Stare at your left fist for a while, and then slowly extend the left thumb, keeping your total attention focused on the act. Then slowly extend the first finger, then your second finger and so on. Now reverse the process, completely focusing on the act, until your fist is back in the original position. Repeat with the right hand. Continue this exercise five times increasing it to ten times.

This is important; by training your attention directing it to a trivial and simple task. You will soon feel the benefit. You will notice that you have much better control over your muscular movements and you will also notice an increased power of attention and concentration, which will give you an advantage in your everyday affairs.

This next class of exercise is intended to help you in concentrating your attention on a material object not connected with yourself. Take some uninteresting object, such as a pen or pencil, and concentrate your entire attention on it for five minutes. Look at it intently like it is your life purpose. Think of nothing else but that pen or pencil. Imagine that there is nothing else in the world except you and this object. Do not let your attention get away from it for a minimum of **5 minutes**.

"There is only one world, but two things in it, pencil and me." You will realize, what a rebellious creature your attention is, but do not let it get the upper hand of you. This will wear that little creature down, but it is for its own good. When you have conquered this rebellious attention, you will have achieved a great victory. An enhanced mind ability which will serve you in any task you set out to do in your daily life.

This exercise can be varied each day, but make sure that you choose an object that is uninteresting. An interesting object requires no effort to concentrate on. You need something that will seem like "work" to the attention; for, the less interesting the object, the more work, and the better the exercise.

4: Enzymes (*Food for Thought*)

Did human disease begin when man started cooking his food?

For example, the Neanderthal man of 50,000 years ago used fire extensively in his cooking. He lived in caves and ate mostly roasted meat from the continuous fires which warmed the caves. From fossil evidences, we know that the Neanderthal man suffered from fully-developed crippling arthritis.

It's possible that the Neanderthal man also had diabetes or cancer or kidney disease and so forth. However, we'll never know since all soft tissues have disappeared without a trace.

Incidentally, another inhabitant of the caves was the cave bear. This creature protected the Neanderthal man from the cave tiger, who also wanted the protection of the cave to avoid the frigid weather. The cave bear, according to paleontologists, was a partially domesticated animal and most likely lived on the same roasted meat that the cave man ate. Like the cave man, the cave bear also suffered from chronic, deforming arthritis.

Consider the primitive Eskimo. He lived in an environment just as frigid as that of the Neanderthal Man. Yet, the Eskimo never suffered from arthritis and other chronic diseases. However, the Eskimo ate large amounts of raw food. The meat he ate was only slightly heated and was raw in the center. Therefore, the Eskimo received a large quantity of food enzymes with every meal. In fact, the word Eskimo itself comes from an Indian expression which means, "He who eats it raw."

Incidentally, there is no tradition of medicine men among the Eskimo people. But among groups like the North American Indian, who ate cooked food extensively, the medicine man had a prominent position in the tribe. Just about every single person eats a diet of mainly cooked foods. Keep in mind that whenever a food is boiled at 212 degrees, the enzymes in it are 100% destroyed.

What is an enzyme? The majority of us never even give a thought to enzymes, yet without them our bodies could not carry out their most basic functions. In their role as organic catalysts, enzymes make possible the millions of biochemical reactions that take place within us daily. They are the powerful engines that drive every bodily process, including breathing and circulation. They digest food, transport nutrients, carry away toxic wastes, purify the blood, deliver hormones, balance cholesterol and triglycerides, nourish the brain, build protein into muscle, and feed and fortify the endocrine system. On a larger scale, enzymes slow the aging process and support wellness and homeostasis (the body's ability to achieve balance.)

Also, we know that decreased enzyme levels are found in a number of chronic ailments, such as allergies, skin disease, and even serious diseases like diabetes and cancer. Food enzyme deficiency may be the cause of the exaggerated maturation of today's children and teenagers. It is also an important cause of obesity in many children and adults. This shows that vitamins and minerals alone are not sufficient for health.

Civilized people eat such large quantities of cooked foods that their enzyme systems are kept busy digesting food. As a result, the body lacks the enzymes needed to maintain the tissues in good health.

Joseph & Jennifer Gamboa

Dogs, for instance, also secrete no enzymes in their saliva when they're eating a raw diet. However, if you start giving them cooked starchy food, their salivary glands will start producing starch-digesting enzymes within 10 days. Enzymes in saliva represent a pathological and not a normal situation. Salivary enzymes cannot digest raw starch.

Exercise 4:

This exercise is intended to elevate your awareness of bringing the body in optimal balance with the mind. They are inseparable and require continuous re-training and recreating. Keep the Power of Sunlight in mind. Store its energy within your cells.

Cooked foods cause such a large drain on our enzyme supply that you can't make it up by eating raw foods. In addition, vegetables and fruits are not concentrated sources of enzymes. When produce ripens, enzymes are present to do the ripening. However, once the ripening is finished, some of the enzymes leave and go back into the stem and seeds.

Changing one's diet and using digestive enzymes are two great strategies to help detoxify the body or return it to a state of balance, or homeostasis. If you want to have a healthy toxin-free body, it is important to stay away from certain foods.

This "stealing" of enzymes from other parts of the body to service the digestive tract sets up a competition for enzymes among the various organ systems and tissues of the body. The resulting metabolic dislocations may be the direct cause of cancer, coronary heart disease, diabetes, and many other chronic incurable diseases. This state of enzyme deficiency stress exists in the majority of persons on the civilized, enzyme-free diet.

The only solution is to take capsules of concentrated plant enzymes. In the absence of contraindications, you should take from 1 to 3 capsules per meal. Of course, if you are eating all raw foods, then no enzymes will be necessary at that meal.

88

The capsules should be opened and sprinkled on the food or chewed with the meal. This way, the enzymes can go to work immediately. Incidentally, taking extra enzymes is the third way to neutralize the enzyme inhibitors in un-sprouted seeds and nuts.

Concentrates of plant enzymes or fungus enzymes are better for pre-digestion of food than tablets of pancreatic enzymes. This is because plant enzymes can work in the acidity of the stomach, whereas pancreatic enzymes only work best in the alkalinity of the small intestine.

Bananas, avocadoes and mangoes are good sources that are high in enzymes. Be aware of enzyme inhibitors such as raw seeds and raw nuts. Therefore, when you eat raw seeds or raw nuts, you are swallowing enzyme inhibitors which will neutralize some of the enzymes your body produces.

First, incorporate at least two, organic raw foods into your daily diet. Make sure that you check for the quality of the freshness, for the essential nutrients will escape over time and exposure; considering the time it takes to package and distribute it to the marketplace.

If you do not own one, invest in a good Juicer, or borrow one from a friend for **5 days.** Most likely, your friend or neighbor has not used it in a while. Prepare **4 organic Granny Smith** apples by slicing them to size to fit in the juicer. Prepare **5 organic** carrots to fit in the juicer. This preparation will minimize the time the nutrients can escape the exposed items. You may add celery or broccoli as well. This will make sixteen ounces, without all of the fiber and starches. Shake well. Immediately drink **8 ounces** and **8 ounces** exactly one hour from the first juice. If you are diabetic, you may want to consider eating them raw or cooked for you will need the fiber to neutralize the sugar.

Take Full Spectrum Digestive Enzymes

Another important factor in creating and maintaining a healthy immune system is to repair and minimize the toxic burden that assaults our bodies every day in the modern industrialized world.

When toxins assault us, or build up in the body, the immune system's capacity to protect us can be overwhelmed. Food allergies are often the result of these insults.

5: Character *(Thought-Absorption)*

The human brain does not know what is real or what is unreal. The neurons will transmit the exact signals based on what you convince your mind to believe. You can *will* a thought into your mind until you believe it, and corresponding, your body and actions will follow and then carry you in that intended direction. We will refer to this as Thought Absorption. Impressing any given thought upon your mind until it is assimilated into your brain and running through your veins. Like a repeated drop of water, it will eventually wear down the stone.

Thought Absorption is an ideal way to develop Character. If practiced and persisted, it will accomplish the most obvious results in a comparatively short space of time, the effect being felt from the start.

In the following exercise, we will use Fear, (worry) thought-habit, as an illustration. It affords an excellent illustration of a bad habit of thought. It does more harm to life than all of the other bad thoughts combined. It is the exact opposite of Love. It also brings with it a filthy host of miserable weakening thought-habits of which it is the parent. The one who tears out these fear thoughts by the roots is on the road to Freedom. Fear thoughts have wrecked the careers and relationships of millions of men and women, paralyzing their energies, preventing their progress, disabling their minds, and diseasing their bodies. We have all felt it, and those of us who have banished it would not return to its control under any consideration.

Life is entirely different to those who root out this noxious weed. They become an entirely different order of being. Most of the things we fear never occur. The energy and vital force wasted on worry is more than enough energy to enable us to conquer our real troubles when they occur. There is a tale of an old man on his death-bed, giving his own son good advice, who said: "John, I have lived eighty years, and I have had many troubles, *the majority of which never occurred.*" The old man merely voiced the experience of all men and women who have lived to old age. The point is obvious.

Exercise 5:

First, you will build the power of the Will, by standing in front of a mirror and say to yourself "I am becoming more and more courageous," "I command fear to depart." Repeat these **20 times.**

Next, use the power of auto-suggestion, or affirmations, by constantly repeating to yourself the words; "I am Powerful; I am Confident; I have abolished fear;" "I have power over all of my emotions." Say it as if you were saying it to another person. Perform this up to **5 minutes a day.** You may say this while you are waiting at a traffic light, or while preparing dinner. It is important to verbalize it out loud. This will activate the vibrations.

Let your passive mind see that you believe what you say, it will deliver confidence in your statements, and, accepting them as correct, it will act accordingly. If you go about this practice in good faith and seriousness, you will notice benefits from the beginning. You must remember, however, that if the Passive mind thrusts a worry upon your consciousness, you must double up on your assertion of Fearlessness, until the intruder retreats. Fear and worry will soon learn that you carry a club, and will beat a hasty retreat at the mere sight of it. Don't wait until he actually bothers you, but get into the habit of reaching for the club at the first sight.

Now you are ready to try the effects of Thought Absorption. Place yourself in a suggestible, passive condition; quiet every nerve, relax every muscle and assume a mental state of calm. The more passive you become, the better the effect will be. Relax and let go of your body and mind. Relieve the Active mind from duty and allow the Passive mind to have control.

You then carry the thoughts of "I am Powerful," and the others above, calmly and firmly. Picture yourself as being powerful, acting powerful, having moral and physical courage, and driving away fear and worry with your club. Give your imagination full scope, but hold it down to the desired line of thought. This is where the Concentration exercises will become important. You will carry the thought of power with you all the time, and endeavor to act the part *naturally*. Act the part just as the actor does when he assumes a role. The assumed character will soon become more real and in time, will be the "real thing" within you. It will soon become second nature to you, and eventually will become your true real *nature*. The true character of a man is not measured in his success, but in the face of adversity.

The above exercises now can be practiced more intelligently, now that you understand the advantages by mental focus and concentration. This being understood, you can extend these Natural Intelligence Applications by your own environment and creativity. You may practice upon something occurring in your everyday work, your business, your choice of recreation, and your relationships.

You will be able to carry the thought better, to direct more energy into suggestions, and into the projection of thought vibrations. You will be able to overcome bad habits and acquire good habits in their place. You will have acquired a firm control over body and mind, and find that you are the master of your thoughts, not their slave. You will get the good things in life starting with self-control, peace of mind and be less rattled by others actions and then the other tangible things you focus on will follow. Remember once you have made positive changes in your life please remember to pay it forward. Help make someone else's hour, day, or life better. May love and peace be your guiding light.

EXERCISES

EXERCISE 1 BREATH

Day One: Date/_____   Minutes/_____

Thought/_____

_____

Day Two: Date/_____   Minutes/_____

Thought/_____

_____

Day Three: Date/_____   Minutes/_____

Thought/_____

_____

Day Four: Date/_____   Minutes/_____

Thought/_____

_____

Day Five: Date/_____   Minutes/_____

Thought/_____

_____

Notes:_____

_____

_____

_____

_____

_____

_____

_____

_____

_____

_____

_____

_____

_____

_____

_____

_____

_____

_____

_____

_____

_____

_____

_____

_____

_____

_____

_____

_____

_____

EXERCISE 2 WATER

Day One: Date/_____   Music/_____
Method/ *Love-Gratitude*_____
_____

Day Two: Date/_____   Music/_____
Method/_____
_____

Day Three: Date/_____   Music/_____
Method/_____
_____

Day Four: Date/_____   Music/_____
Method/_____
_____

Day Five: Date/_____   Music/_____
Method/_____
_____

Notes:

EXERCISE 3 CENTER

Day One: Date/_____   Involuntary (mins)/_____
Voluntary/(mins)   Object/_____
Thought/_____

Day Two: Date/_____   Invol/_____
Vol/_____   Object _____
_____

Day Three: Date/_____   Invol/_____
Vol/_____   Object _____
_____

Day Four: Date/_____   Invol/_____
Vol/_____   Object _____
_____

Day Five: Date/_____   Invol/_____
Vol/_____   Object _____
_____

Notes:_____

EXERCISE 4 ENZYMES

Day One: Date/_____   Juice(qty)/_____
Food type/_____
Normal food avoided/_____

Day Two: Date/_____   Juice/_____
Food type/_____
Avoids/ _____

Day Three: Date/_____   Juice/_____
Food type/_____
Avoids/ _____

Day Four: Date/_____   Juice/_____
Food type/_____
Avoids/ _____

Day Five: Date/_____   Juice/_____
Food type/_____
Avoids/ _____

Notes:

Exercise 5 Thought Absorption

Day One: Date/_____   I let go of Fear/_____(x)

I am Powerful/_____(x) I am Confident/_____(x)

I am/_____(x) I am/_____(x)

Day Two: Date/_____   I let go of Fear/_____(x)

I am Powerful/_____(x) I am Confident/_____(x)

I am/_____(x) I am/_____(x)

Day Three: Date/_____   I let go of Fear/_____(x)

I am Powerful/_____(x) I am Confident/_____(x)

I am/_____(x) I am/_____(x)

Day Four: Date/_____   I let go of Fear/_____(x)

I am Powerful/_____(x) I am Confident/_____(x)

I am/_____(x) I am/_____(x)

Day Five: Date/_____   I let go of Fear/_____(x)

I am Powerful/_____(x) I am Confident/_____(x)

I am/_____(x) I am/_____(x)

Notes:

EXERCISE 1 BREATH

Day One: Date/_____   Minutes/_____
Thought/_____
_____

Day Two: Date/_____   Minutes/_____
Thought/_____
_____

Day Three: Date/_____   Minutes/_____
Thought/_____
_____

Day Four: Date/_____   Minutes/_____
Thought/_____
_____

Day Five: Date/_____   Minutes/_____
Thought/_____
_____

Notes:_____

_____
_____
_____
_____
_____
_____
_____
_____
_____
_____
_____
_____
_____
_____
_____
_____
_____
_____
_____
_____
_____
_____
_____
_____
_____
_____
_____
_____
_____

EXERCISE 2 WATER

Day One: Date/_____   Music/_____
Method/ *Love-Gratitude*_____

_____

Day Two: Date/_____   Music/_____
Method/_____

_____

Day Three: Date/_____   Music/_____
Method/_____

_____

Day Four: Date/_____   Music/_____
Method/_____

_____

Day Five: Date/_____   Music/_____
Method/_____

_____

Notes:_____

_____

_____

_____

_____

_____

_____

_____

_____

_____

_____

_____

_____

_____

_____

_____

_____

_____

_____

_____

_____

_____

_____

_____

_____

_____

_____

_____

_____

_____

_____

_____

_____

EXERCISE 3 CENTER

Day One: Date/_____   Involuntary (mins)/_____
Voluntary/(mins)   Object/_____
Thought/_____

Day Two: Date/_____   Invol/_____
Vol/_____   Object _____
_____

Day Three: Date/_____   Invol/_____
Vol/_____   Object _____
_____

Day Four: Date/_____   Invol/_____
Vol/_____   Object _____
_____

Day Five: Date/_____   Invol/_____
Vol/_____   Object _____
_____

Notes:

EXERCISE 4 ENZYMES

Day One: Date/_____   Juice(qty)/_____
Food type/_____
Normal food avoided/_____

Day Two: Date/_____   Juice/_____
Food type/_____
Avoids/ _____

Day Three: Date/_____   Juice/_____
Food type/_____
Avoids/ _____

Day Four: Date/_____   Juice/_____
Food type/_____
Avoids/ _____

Day Five: Date/_____   Juice/_____
Food type/_____
Avoids/ _____

Notes:

EXERCISE 5 THOUGHT ABSORPTION

Day One: Date/_____   I let go of Fear/_____(x)
I am Powerful/_____(x) I am Confident/_____(x)
I am/_____(x) I am/_____(x)

Day Two: Date/_____   I let go of Fear/_____(x)
I am Powerful/_____(x) I am Confident/_____(x)
I am/_____(x) I am/_____(x)

Day Three: Date/_____   I let go of Fear/_____(x)
I am Powerful/_____(x) I am Confident/_____(x)
I am/_____(x) I am/_____(x)

Day Four: Date/_____   I let go of Fear/_____(x)
I am Powerful/_____(x) I am Confident/_____(x)
I am/_____(x) I am/_____(x)

Day Five: Date/_____   I let go of Fear/_____(x)
I am Powerful/_____(x) I am Confident/_____(x)
I am/_____(x) I am/_____(x)

Notes:

EXERCISE 1 BREATH

Day One: Date/_____   Minutes/_____
Thought/_____
_____

Day Two: Date/_____   Minutes/_____
Thought/_____
_____

Day Three: Date/_____   Minutes/_____
Thought/_____
_____

Day Four: Date/_____   Minutes/_____
Thought/_____
_____

Day Five: Date/_____   Minutes/_____
Thought/_____
_____

Notes:

EXERCISE 2 WATER

Day One: Date/_____   Music/_____
Method/ *Love-Gratitude*_____
_____

Day Two: Date/_____   Music/_____
Method/_____
_____

Day Three: Date/_____   Music/_____
Method/_____
_____

Day Four: Date/_____   Music/_____
Method/_____
_____

Day Five: Date/_____   Music/_____
Method/_____
_____

Notes:

EXERCISE 3 CENTER

Day One: Date/_____   Involuntary (mins)/_____

Voluntary/(mins) Object/_____

Thought/_____

Day Two: Date/_____   Invol/_____

Vol/_____   Object _____

_____

Day Three: Date/_____   Invol/_____

Vol/_____   Object _____

_____

Day Four: Date/_____   Invol/_____

Vol/_____   Object _____

_____

Day Five: Date/_____   Invol/_____

Vol/_____   Object _____

_____

Notes:

EXERCISE 4 ENZYMES

Day One: Date/_____   Juice(qty)/_____
Food type/_____
Normal food avoided/_____

Day Two: Date/_____   Juice/_____
Food type/_____
Avoids/ _____

Day Three: Date/_____   Juice/_____
Food type/_____
Avoids/ _____

Day Four: Date/_____   Juice/_____
Food type/_____
Avoids/ _____

Day Five: Date/_____   Juice/_____
Food type/_____
Avoids/ _____

Notes:_____

_____
_____
_____
_____
_____
_____
_____
_____
_____
_____
_____
_____
_____
_____
_____
_____
_____
_____
_____
_____
_____
_____
_____
_____
_____
_____
_____
_____
_____
_____
_____
_____
_____

Exercise 5 Thought Absorption

Day One: Date/_____   I let go of Fear/_____(x)
I am Powerful/_____(x)   I am Confident/_____(x)
I am/_____(x)   I am/_____(x)

Day Two: Date/_____   I let go of Fear/_____(x)
I am Powerful/_____(x)   I am Confident/_____(x)
I am/_____(x)   I am/_____(x)

Day Three: Date/_____   I let go of Fear/_____(x)
I am Powerful/_____(x)   I am Confident/_____(x)
I am/_____(x)   I am/_____(x)

Day Four: Date/_____   I let go of Fear/_____(x)
I am Powerful/_____(x)   I am Confident/_____(x)
I am/_____(x)   I am/_____(x)

Day Five: Date/_____   I let go of Fear/_____(x)
I am Powerful/_____(x)   I am Confident/_____(x)
I am/_____(x)   I am/_____(x)

Notes:

Exercise 1 Breath

Day One: Date/_____   Minutes/_____

Thought/_____

_____

Day Two: Date/_____   Minutes/_____

Thought/_____

_____

Day Three: Date/_____   Minutes/_____

Thought/_____

_____

Day Four: Date/_____   Minutes/_____

Thought/_____

_____

Day Five: Date/_____   Minutes/_____

Thought/_____

_____

Notes:_____

_____

_____

_____

_____

_____

_____

_____

_____

_____

_____

_____

_____

_____

_____

_____

_____

_____

_____

_____

_____

_____

_____

_____

_____

_____

_____

_____

_____

_____

_____

_____

_____

_____

Day One: Date/_____   Music/_____
Method/ *Love-Gratitude*_____

_____

Day Two: Date/_____   Music/_____
Method/_____

_____

Day Three: Date/_____   Music/_____
Method/_____

_____

Day Four: Date/_____   Music/_____
Method/_____

_____

Day Five: Date/_____   Music/_____
Method/_____

_____

Notes:

EXERCISE 3 CENTER

Day One: Date/_____   Involuntary (mins)/_____
Voluntary/(mins) Object/_____
Thought/_____

Day Two: Date/_____   Invol/_____
Vol/_____   Object _____
_____

Day Three: Date/_____   Invol/_____
Vol/_____   Object _____
_____

Day Four: Date/_____   Invol/_____
Vol/_____   Object _____
_____

Day Five: Date/_____   Invol/_____
Vol/_____   Object _____
_____

Notes:

EXERCISE 4 ENZYMES

Day One: Date/_____   Juice(qty)/_____
Food type/_____
Normal food avoided/_____

Day Two: Date/_____   Juice/_____
Food type/_____
Avoids/ _____

Day Three: Date/_____   Juice/_____
Food type/_____
Avoids/ _____

Day Four: Date/_____   Juice/_____
Food type/_____
Avoids/ _____

Day Five: Date/_____   Juice/_____
Food type/_____
Avoids/ _____

Notes:

EXERCISE 5 THOUGHT ABSORPTION

Day One: Date/_____   I let go of Fear/_____(x)
I am Powerful/_____(x)   I am Confident/_____(x)
I am/_____(x)   I am/_____(x)

Day Two: Date/_____   I let go of Fear/_____(x)
I am Powerful/_____(x)   I am Confident/_____(x)
I am/_____(x)   I am/_____(x)

Day Three: Date/_____   I let go of Fear/_____(x)
I am Powerful/_____(x)   I am Confident/_____(x)
I am/_____(x)   I am/_____(x)

Day Four: Date/_____   I let go of Fear/_____(x)
I am Powerful/_____(x)   I am Confident/_____(x)
I am/_____(x)   I am/_____(x)

Day Five: Date/_____   I let go of Fear/_____(x)
I am Powerful/_____(x)   I am Confident/_____(x)
I am/_____(x)   I am/_____(x)

Notes:
_____

ABOUT THE AUTHOR

Joseph Gamboa was sought out to attend Boston Latin because of his outstanding junior high academics and good citizenship. Joseph attended Boston Latin from grade 7-12. After successfully graduating high school, Joe joined the armed forces as a Marine and was honorably discharged as a Lance Corporal. He began an entry level job at a company in Seattle, Washington and after achieving senior status; Joseph bought the company and caused it to succeed even further until he eventually sold the company and retired at age 36. Joseph returned to pursue a higher education to follow his dream in film school at Brooks Institute of Photography. He continued to follow his boyhood dream of being an entrepreneur inspired by his beloved father.

Joe was fortunate enough to travel to all the states in the USA, except Alaska and Puerto Rico. Joseph was also blessed to be able to travel to various countries. Joe has a 159 IQ. His soft heart allowed him the great opportunity of being a nurturing father of two daughters and a loving, serving, attentive, loyal husband and leader of his family. He continued to teach anyone willing to listen with the hopes to one day receive the Nobel Peace Prize. Joseph was very successful, he owned luxury custom cars (4 at a time), had the 90-degree lake view home but after many years; he started to study minimalism and started to let go of the ego based items in life and go after inner peace. For at least 14 years, Joe was dedicated to working out daily, eating healthy and meditating.

With Love, Respect, and Dedication to a man so admired and loved by others. I dedicate this section to the Best Man I know, my husband and the love of my life.

Jennifer Gamboa

Printed in the United States
By Bookmasters